Boo!

GHOSTS AND GRAVES

Boo!

Kevin Crossley-Holland

Illustrated by
Peter Melnyczuk

ORCHARD BOOKS
London

Text copyright © Kevin Crossley-Holland 1988
"Bold as Brass" first appeared as "The Dauntless
Girl" in *The Dead Moon* (André Deutsch 1982).
Illustrations copyright © Peter Melnyczuk 1988
First published in Great Britain in 1988 by
ORCHARD BOOKS
10 Golden Square, London W1R 3AF
Orchard Books Australia
14 Mars Road, Lane Cove NSW 2066
Orchard Books Canada
20 Torbay Road, Markham, Ontario 23P 1G6
1 85213 091 1
Typeset in Great Britain by
Tradespools Ltd, Frome, Somerset
Printed in Great Britain by A Wheaton, Exeter

Contents

Her

I was standing on the footbridge when I saw her coming. The summer water drifted under the bridge and she slid up towards me wearing a white cotton dress, high neck, long sleeves.

Here's a nice young thing, I thought, and I can't say I've ever seen her before. But whoever she is, I'll give her a fright.

I just stood and waited for her to drift up to me, stood and waited in the middle of the bridge. And when she came close, all of a sudden I reached out and wrapped my arms around her—like this!

She wasn't there!

Billy

Billy wasn't born a cripple. He fell out of the apple tree when he was four and broke both his legs. He broke them in several places.

There was no doctor within a day's ride of the village, so the two wise women laid poor Billy on a table, and prepared splints, and set his legs as best they could. The legs set crooked, though, very crooked, and from that day forward Billy was unable to walk.

While his friends played chase and turned cartwheels, and flexed their lengthening limbs, all Billy could do was haul himself along on a pair of crutches. Everyone liked him though. They had no end of time for him because he was cheerful and brave, and made the most of his life. His friends always carted him round to their games and gatherings.

When he grew up, Billy became a tailor. The little cripple sat cross-legged in his cottage surrounded by bright rings of talk and laughter. And after supper, he used to swing along on his sticks in the direction of the village pub.

One Hallowe'en, while Billy and his friends were sitting in the pub, a band of tricksters burst in with howls and shouts. The boys wore girls' clothing, the girls wore shirts and trousers, and all their faces were blackened with soot. At once they blew out the publican's two paraffin lamps, which stood at each end of the bar, and then they swung their own turnip lanterns in front of the drinkers.

Billy and his friends stared at the swinging faces—their fiery eyes and rough-cut mouths, their glow and flicker. And later, when the tricksters had been given food and drink and gone on their way, leaving behind them an aftertow of quiet and emptiness, the publican said: "That's scared off the ghosts, then."

A log hissed and spat in the grate.

"There'll be ghosts in the church-yard, though," said a voice.

"That's no place to be tonight," another voice exclaimed.

"I'm not frit!" said Billy quickly.

"The churchyard," said the pub-lican. "That's alive tonight . . ."

"I'm not frit," said Billy again. "I'll go to the churchyard. I'll sit and sew there all night."

Laughing and alert, Billy's friends carried him back to his cottage to collect cloth and needle and thread; then they took one of the farmer's

carts and rolled the cripple up the hill to the graveyard.

"Come on, Billy!" said a voice.

"See you in the morning, Billy," said several voices.

In the moonlight the tailor sat down on a flagstone, and spread out his cloth. It was so bright that he could see to sew. Billy sewed until eleven o'clock, and sewed until twelve o'clock . . .

Then Billy heard a rumble of a voice from the headstone right behind him. The grave began to open and Billy was showered with fistfuls of sand. Out came a head and the head thundered, "Do you see this head without flesh or blood?"

"Yes," said the tailor, "I see that, but I sew this."

"Do you see this arm without flesh or blood?"

"Yes," said the tailor, "I see that, but I sew this."

"Do you see this body without flesh or blood?"

"Yes," said the tailor, "I see that, but I sew this."

15

By now a huge man, eight foot tall, had come out of the grave. As he started to speak again, Billy finished his piece of sewing; he raised the cloth to his mouth and bit off the thread.

Then the thing reached out and clawed at Billy with its huge bone-hand.

The little tailor leaped up. He pelted across the churchyard and jumped right over the wall.

"Do you see this? Do you see this?" shouted the tailor. And he ran all the way home, laughing.

King of the Cats

I suppose I can think myself lucky. There's plenty in our village who are drawing unemployment, and I know two more—three if you count Dan, he's taking early retirement—who reckon they'll be laid off before Christmas. At least people need me; and they always will.

It's not all laughs, mind. The only ones who thank you are the early birds. And then you're all on your own, and you're out in every weather, too. And the old flowers, the pulpy heaps of them, they smell sickly sweet!

You get some weird experiences, I can tell you. Weird and wonderful!

One evening last summer, I was digging late; the vicar said they needed the grave for nine in the morning. I was having my break, sitting on the edge like, and swinging my legs. Well, I took a nip or two and I was so tired that I reckon I fell asleep.

A cat woke me up, "Miaou!" And when I opened my eyes, it was almost dark and I was down at the bottom.

I stood up and peered over the edge and you know what I saw? Nine black cats! They all had white chests and they were coming down the path, carrying a coffin covered with black velvet. My! Oh my! I kept very quiet but I still had a careful look. There was a little gold crown sitting on top of the black velvet. And at every third step the cats all paused, solemn like, and cried "Miaou!"

21

Then the cats turned off the path and headed straight towards me. Their eyes were shining, luminous and green. Eight of them were carrying the coffin and a big one walked in front of them, showing them the way. One step, two steps, three steps: miaou!

When they got to the graveside, they stopped. They all looked straight at me. My! Oh my! I felt queer.

Then the big cat, the one at the front, stepped towards me. "Tell Dildrum," he said in a squeaky voice, "tell Dildrum," he said, "that Doldrum is dead."

Then he turned his back on me and led away the other cats with the coffin. One step, two steps, three steps: miaou!

As soon as they were out of the

way, I scrambled out of the grave,
and I was glad to get home, I can
tell you. There they all were: my
Mary cross-eyed with knitting and

24

Mustard hopping around his cage and old Sam stretched out in the corner. Everything as usual; the clock ticking on the mantelpiece.

So I told the old girl about the talking cat and the coffin and the crown. She gave me one of those looks—a sort of gleam behind her specs.

"Yes, Harry," she said.

"It's true, Mary," I said. "I couldn't have made it up. And who is Dildrum anyhow?"

"How should I know?" said Mary. "That's enough of your

stories. You're upsetting old Sam."

Old Sam got up. First he prowled around and then he looked straight at me. My! Oh my! I felt very queer again.

"That's just what the cat said," I said. "Not a word more and not a word less. He said, 'Tell Dildrum that Doldrum is dead.' But how can I? How can I tell Dildrum that Doldrum is dead if I don't know who Dildrum is?"

"Stop, Harry!" shouted Mary. "Look at old Sam! Look!"

Old Sam was sort of swelling. Swelling and staring right through me. And at last he shrieked out, "Doldrum—old Doldrum dead? Then I'm the King of the Cats!"

He leaped into the fireplace and up the chimney, and he has never been seen again.

Bold as Brass

"Dang it!" said the farmer. "Not a drop left."

"Not one?" asked the blacksmith, raising his glass and inspecting it. His last inch of whisky glowed like molten honey in the flickering firelight.

"Why not?" said the miller.

"You fool!" said the farmer. "Because the bottle's empty." He peered into the flames. "Never mind that though," he said. "We'll

send out my Mary. She'll go down to the inn and bring us another bottle."

"What?" said the blacksmith. "She'll be afraid to go out on such a dark night, all the way down to the village, and all on her own."

"Never!" said the farmer. "She's afraid of nothing—nothing live or dead. She's worth all my lads put together."

The farmer gave a shout and Mary came out of the kitchen. She stood and she listened. She went out into the dark night and in a little time returned with another bottle of whisky.

The miller and the blacksmith were delighted. They drank to her health, but later the miller said, "That's a strange thing, though."

"What's that?" asked the farmer.

"That she should be so bold, your Mary."

"Bold as brass," said the blacksmith. "Out and alone and the night so dark."

"That's nothing at all," said the farmer. "She'd go anywhere, day or night. She's afraid of nothing—nothing live or dead."

"Words," said the blacksmith. "But my, this whisky tastes good."

"Words nothing," said the farmer. "I bet you a golden guinea that neither of you can name anything that girl will not do."

The miller scratched his head and the blacksmith peered at the golden guinea of whisky in his glass. "All right," said the blacksmith. "Let's meet here again at the same time next week. Then I'll name something Mary will not do."

Next week the blacksmith went to see the priest and borrowed the key of the church door from him. Then he paid a visit to the sexton—the old man who rang the church bells and dug the graves—and showed him the key.

"What do you want with that?" asked the sexton.

"What I want with you," said the blacksmith, "is this. I want you to go into the church tonight, just before midnight, and hide yourself in the dead house."

"Never," said the sexton.

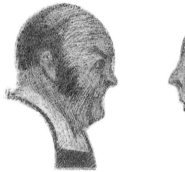

"Not for half a guinea?" asked the blacksmith.

The old sexton's eyes popped out of his head. "Dang it!" he said. "What's that for then?"

"To frighten that farm girl, Mary," said the blacksmith, grinning. "She's bold as brass. When she comes to the dead house, you just give a moan or a holler."

The old sexton's desire for the half guinea was even greater than his fear. He hummed and hawed and at last agreed to do as the blacksmith asked.

Then the blacksmith clumped the sexton on the back with his massive fist and the old sexton coughed. "I'll see you tomorrow," said the blacksmith, "and settle the account. Just before midnight, then! Not a minute later!"

The sexton nodded and the blacksmith strode up to the farm. Darkness was falling and the farmer and the miller were already drinking and waiting for him.

"Well?" said the farmer.

The blacksmith grasped his glass, then raised it and rolled the whisky around his mouth.

"Well," said the farmer. "Are you or aren't you?"

"This," said the blacksmith, "is what your Mary will not do. She won't go into the church alone at midnight. . ."

"No," said the miller.

". . . and go to the dead house," continued the blacksmith, "and bring back a skull bone. That's what she won't do."

"Never," said the miller.

The farmer gave a shout and

Mary came out of the kitchen. She stood and listened; and later, at midnight, she went out into the darkness and walked down to the church.

Mary opened the church door. She held up her lamp and clattered down the steps to the dead house. She pushed open its creaking door and saw skulls and thigh bones and bones of every kind gleaming in front of her. She stooped and picked up the nearest skull bone.

"Let that be," moaned a muffled voice from behind the dead house door. "That's my mother's skull bone."

So Mary put that skull down and picked up another.

"Let that be," moaned a muffled voice from behind the dead house door. "That's my father's skull bone."

So Mary put that skull bone down too and picked up yet another one. And, as she did so, she angrily called out, "Father or mother, sister or brother, I *must* have a skull bone and that's my last word." Then she walked out of the dead house, slammed the door, and hurried up the steps and back up to the farm.

Mary put the skull bone on the table in front of the farmer. "There's your skull bone, master," she said, and started off for the kitchen.

"Wait a minute!" said the farmer, grinning and shivering at one and the same time. "Didn't you hear anything in the dead house, Mary?"

"Yes," she said. "Some fool of a ghost called out to me: 'Let that be! That's my mother's skull bone' and 'Let that be! That's my father's skull bone.' But I told him straight: 'Father or mother, sister or brother, I *must* have a skull bone.'"

The miller and the blacksmith stared at Mary and shook their heads.

"So I took one," said Mary, "and here I am and here it is." She looked down at the three faces flickering in the firelight. "As I was going away," she said, "after I had locked the door, I heard the old ghost hollering and shrieking like mad."

The blacksmith and the miller looked at each other and got to their feet.

"That'll do then, Mary," said the farmer.

The blacksmith knew that the sexton must have been scared out of his wits at being locked all alone in the dead house. They all raced

down to the church, and clattered down the steps into the dead house, but they were too late. They found the old man lying stone dead on his face.

"That's what comes of trying to frighten a poor young girl," said the farmer. So the blacksmith gave the farmer a golden guinea and the farmer gave it to his Mary.

Mary and her daring were known in every house. And after her visit to the dead house, and the death of the old sexton, her fame spread for miles and miles around.

One day the squire, who lived three villages off, rode up to the farm and asked the farmer if he could talk to Mary.

"I've heard," said the squire, "that you're afraid of nothing."

Mary nodded.

"Nothing live or dead," said the farmer proudly.

"Listen then!" said the squire. "Last year my old mother died and was buried. But she will not rest. She keeps coming back into the house, and especially at mealtimes. Sometimes you can see her, sometimes you can't. And when you can't, you can still see a knife and fork get up off the table and play about where her hands would be."

"That's a strange thing altogether," said the farmer, "that she should go on walking."

"Strange and unnatural," said the squire. "And now my servants won't stay with me, not one of them. They're all afraid of her."

The farmer sighed and shook his head. "Hard to come by, good servants," he said.

"So," said the squire, "seeing as she's afraid of nothing, nothing live or dead, I'd like to ask your girl to come and work with me."

Mary was pleased with the prospect of such good employment and, sorry as he was to lose her, the farmer saw there was nothing for it but to let her go.

"I'll come," said the girl. "I'm not afraid of ghosts. But you ought to take account of that in my wages."

"I will," said the squire.

So Mary went back with the

squire to be his servant. The first
thing she always did was to lay a
place for the ghost at table, and she
took great care not to let the knife
and fork lie criss-cross.

At meals, Mary passed the ghost
the meat and vegetables and sauce
and gravy. And then she said:
"Pepper, madam?" and "Salt,
madam?" The ghost of the squire's
mother was pleased enough.
Things went on the same from day
to day until the squire had to go up
to London to settle some legal busi-
ness.

Next morning Mary was down on her knees, cleaning the parlour grate, when she noticed something thin and glimmering push in through the parlour door, which was just ajar; when it got inside the room, the shape began to swell and open out. It was the old ghost.

For the first time, the ghost spoke

to the girl. "Mary," she said in a hollow voice, "are you afraid of me?"

"No, madam," said Mary. "I've no cause to be afraid of you, for you are dead and I'm alive."

For a while the ghost looked at the girl kneeling by the parlour grate. "Mary," she said, "will you come down into the cellar with me? You mustn't bring a light—but I'll shine enough to light the way for you."

So the two of them went down the cellar steps and the ghost shone like an old lantern. When they got to the bottom, they went down a passage, and took a right turn and a left, and then the ghost pointed to some loose tiles in one corner. "Pick up those tiles," she said.

Mary did as she was asked. And underneath the tiles were two bags of gold, a big one and a little one.

The ghost quivered. "Mary," she said, "that big bag is for your master. But that little bag is for you, for you are a fearless girl and deserve it."

Before Mary could open the bag or even open her mouth, the old

ghost drifted up the steps and out of
sight. She was never seen again and
Mary had a devil of a time groping
her way along the dark passage and
up out of the cellar.

After three days, the squire came
back from London.

"Good morning, Mary," he said. "Have you seen anything of my mother while I've been away?"

"Yes, sir," said Mary. "That I have." She opened her eyes wide. "And if you aren't afraid of coming down into the cellar with me, I'll show you something."

The squire laughed. "I'm not afraid if you're not afraid," he said, for the fearless girl was a very pretty girl.

So Mary lit a candle and led the squire down into the cellar, walked along the passage, took a right turn and a left, and raised the loose tiles in the corner for a second time.

"Two bags," said the squire.

"Two bags of gold," said Mary. "The little one is for you and the big one is for me."

"Lor!" said the squire, and he

said nothing else. He did think that his mother might have given him the big bag, as indeed she had, but all the same he took what he could.

After that, Mary always crossed the knives and forks at mealtimes to prevent the old ghost from telling what she had done.

The squire thought things over: the gold and the ghost and Mary's good looks. What with one thing and another he proposed to Mary, and the fearless girl, she accepted him. In a little while they married, and so the squire did get both bags of gold after all.

Samuel's Ghost

Poor old Samuel! He was asleep when his cottage caught fire, and when he woke up it was too late. He was only a lad and he was burned to death; he got turned into ashes, and maybe cinders.

After a while, though, Samuel got up. The inside of him got up and gave itself a shake. He must have felt rather queer; he wasn't used to doing without a body, and he didn't know what to do next,

and all around him there were bog-
garts and bogles and chancy things,
and he was a bit scared.

Before long, Samuel heard a
voice. "You must go to the graveyard," said whatever it was, "and
tell the Big Worm you're dead."

"Must I?" said Samuel.

"And ask him to have you eaten
up." said the something. "Other-
wise you'll never rest in the earth."

"I'm willing," said Samuel.

So Samuel set off for the graveyard, asking the way of whatever
he met, rubbing shoulders with all

the horrid things that swarmed and scowled around him.

By and by, Samuel came to an empty dark space. Glimmering lights were crossing and recrossing it. It smelt earthy, as strong as the soil in spring, and here and there it gave off a ghastly stink, sickening and scary. Underfoot were creeping things, and all round were crawling, fluttering things, and the air was hot and tacky.

On the far side of this space was a horrid great worm, coiled up on a flat stone, and its slimy head was nodding and swinging from side to side, as if it were sniffing out its dinner.

Samuel was afraid when he heard something call out his name, and the worm shot its horrid head right into his face. "Samuel! Is that you,

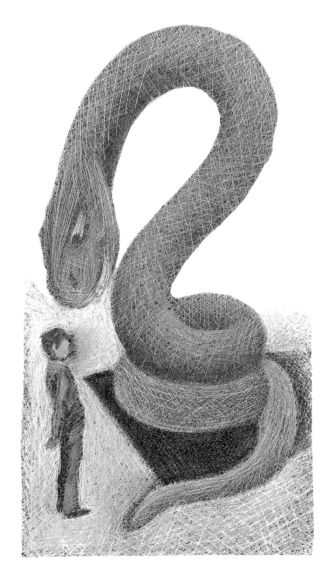

Samuel? So you're dead and buried, and food for the worms, are you?"

"I am," said Samuel.

"Well!" said the worm. "Where's your body?"

"Please, your worship," said Samuel—he didn't want to anger the worm, naturally—"I'm all here!"

"No," said the worm. "How do you think we can eat you? You must fetch your corpse if you want to rest in the earth."

"But where is it?" said Samuel, scratching his head. "My corpse?"

"Where is it buried?" said the worm.

"It isn't buried," said Samuel. "That's just it. It's ashes. I got burned up."

"Ha!" said the worm. "That's bad. That's very bad. You'll not taste too good."

Samuel didn't know what to say.

"Don't fret," said the worm. "Go and fetch the ashes. Bring them here and we'll do all we can."

So Samuel went back to his burned-out cottage. He looked and looked. He scooped up all the ashes he could find into a sack, and took them off to the great worm.

Samuel opened the sack, and the worm crawled down off the flat stone. It sniffed the ashes and turned them over and over.

"Samuel," said the worm after a while. "Something's missing. You're not all here, Samuel. Where's the rest of you? You'll have to find the rest."

"I've brought all I could find," said Samuel.

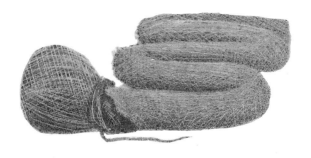

"No," the worm said. "There's an arm missing."

"Ah!" said Samuel. "That's right! I lost an arm I had."

"Lost?" said the worm.

"It was cut off," said Samuel.

"You must find it, Samuel."

Samuel frowned. "I don't know

where the doctor put it," he said. "I can go and see."

So Samuel hurried off again. He hunted high and low, and after a while he found his arm.

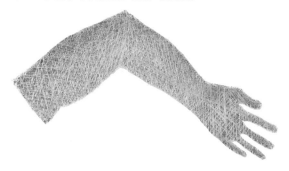

Samuel went straight back to the worm. "Here's the arm," he said.

The worm slid off its flat stone and turned the arm over.

"No, Samuel," said the worm. "There's something still missing. Did you lose anything else?"

"Let's see," said Samuel. "Let's see . . . I lost a nail once, and that never grew again."

"That's it, I reckon!" said the worm. "You've got to find it, Samuel."

"I don't think I'll ever find that, master," said Samuel. "Not one nail. I'll give it a try though."

So Samuel hurried off for the third time. But a nail is just as hard to find as it's easy to lose. Although Samuel searched and searched, he couldn't find anything; so at last he went back to the worm.

"I've searched and searched and I've found nothing," said Samuel. "You must take me without my nail—it's no great loss, is it? Can't you make do without it?"

"No," said the worm. "I can't. And if you can't find it—are you quite certain you can't, Samuel?"

"Certain, worse luck!"

"Then you must walk! You must

walk by day and walk by night. I'm very sorry for you, Samuel, but you'll have plenty of company!"

Then all the creeping things and crawling things swarmed round Samuel and turned him out. And unless he has found it, Samuel has been walking and hunting for his nail from that day to this.

Boo!

She didn't like it at all when her father had to go down to London and, for the first time, she had to sleep alone in the old house.

She went up to her bedroom early. She turned the key and locked the door. She latched the windows and drew the curtains. Then she peered inside her wardrobe, and pulled open the bottom drawer of her clothes press; she got down on her knees and looked under the bed.

She undressed; she put on her nightdress.

She pulled back the heavy linen cover and climbed into bed. Not to read but to try and sleep—she wanted to sleep as soon as she could. She reached out and turned off the lamp.

"That's good," said a little voice. "Now we're safely locked in for the night."